The
Pirate's Secret

READZ●NE

ReadZone Books Limited

2 College Street,
Ludlow,
Shropshire SY8 1AN
www.ReadZoneBooks.com
© in this edition 2015 ReadZone Books Limited

This print edition published in cooperation with Fiction Express, who first published this title in weekly instalments as an interactive e-book.

FICTI●N EXPRESS

Fiction Express
First Floor Office, 2 College Street,
Ludlow, Shropshire SY8 1AN
www.fictionexpress.co.uk

Find out more about Fiction Express on pages 98–99.

Design: Laura Durman & Keith Williams
Cover Image: Shutterstock Images

© in the text 2015 Stewart Ross
The moral right of the author has been asserted.

ISBN 978-1-78322-552-1

Printed in Malta by Melita Press.

To Emily

The
Pirate's Secret

Stewart Ross

Best wishes
[signature]
_2017_

**FICTION
EXPRESS**

What do other readers think?

Here are some comments left on the Fiction Express
blog about this book:

"I love your book The Pirate's Secret.
I can't wait to read the next chapter."
Amy, Cardiff

"I have enjoyed reading The Pirate's Secret
on Fiction Express."
Zahra, Birmingham

*"*The Pirate's Secret *is so amazing"*
Ishmam, Birmingham

"I love this book. It's the best book ever."
Holly, Tweedmouth

*"This book is really imaginative and creative.
It's like a journey come true."*
Lamees, Birmingham

Contents

Chapter 1   Taken!   7

Chapter 2   A Plan   14

Chapter 3   Discovery!   19

Chapter 4   'Traitor Tregorey'   28

Chapter 5   Merciless!   33

Chapter 6   Imprisoned!   43

Chapter 7   A Happy Reunion   58

Chapter 8   The Pit   65

Chapter 9   Betrayed!   76

Chapter 10 The Chase   84

About Fiction Express   98

About the Author   104

Chapter 1

Taken!

I remember it as if it were yesterday. A devil of a sou'westerly was screaming 'round the chimney pots and lashing barrels of rain against our parlour window. Inside, snug before a seacoal fire, father and I sat in silence. I was dreaming of summer sunshine; father, gazing up at his battered brass telescope on the mantelpiece, was reliving his sea days.

I was just about to take myself off to bed, when he lifted his weather-worn face and asked quietly, "Never told you 'bout my secret, has I lad – my…my *golden* secret?"

No, he had not. I was now wide awake and begged him to tell me all about it.

Father smiled, his blue eyes twinkling in the firelight. "Can't tell you every little drop and speck right now, Arden," he said, "seeing as you're not yet quite grown. But one day you'll know all, sure as gulls is gulls – and you'll like what you hears, or my name's not Bill Tregorey! For now, though, you'll have to make do with what I feels is suitable."

Poor father! I know he was trying to do his best by me, but I was annoyed. I understood all about the world, I boasted. Hadn't I managed alright since mother died? Didn't I help him with his work as a cobbler? Couldn't I read letters and numbers as well as any boy in Bedminster?

"So tell me all!" I begged.

Father shook his head. "No, Arden Tregorey. Tough you might be, and almost as sensible as a growed-up. But what I knows ain't fit for someone of your tender years. It might just put you in…in difficulties, you see."

Although I huffed and muttered that he wasn't being fair, I soon got over it when he began his tale. For a full half-hour he spoke of his days as a mariner, of deep blue lagoons and golden sands, of shipwrecks and adventures. The best he saved to the end – how he had outwitted the most dastardly pirate in all the Caribbean.

"His name?" I asked, leaning forward so far that the fire almost singed my hair. "What's his name, father?"

"It's writ as 'Spain'," he replied, speaking in scarcely more than a whisper. "Lambert Spain. But to us seafarers he was always 'Luggole' Spain – he had only one ear, y'see. Other were chopped clean off in a fight. And like I said, your father – plain Bill Tregorey – he got the better of Luggole, he did. I knows the golden secret, and that old pirate would stop at nothing, murder even, to get his hands on it. That's why I ain't told you. But I promise I will one day, Arden my boy. And then you and me will sail the ocean to uncover the secret for ourselves."

He chuckled – but there was little happiness in the sound. Later, lying in bed and listening to the storm gradually subsiding outside, I realized why. After all those years, father was afraid…still afraid of Luggole Spain.

* * *

My father's fear became a horrible reality the very next day. We rose at cockcrow and, splashing through the puddles that made our village street more of a ditch than a road, I set off for market. We needed more hobnails for the soles of the boots father made, and I wanted to sell the half-a-dozen belts I had fashioned from leftover pieces of leather.

I wasn't gone long, but the moment I turned the corner by the church on my way home I knew something was wrong. A small crowd had gathered round our house. As I approached, I saw the front door had been knocked off its hinges. Seeing me, the crowd fell silent as a funeral.

It was Mrs Willerby, the baker's wife, who eventually spoke. About an hour after first light, she said, a gang of five or six ruffians – all seafaring men by the look of them – had smashed their way into the workroom at the front of our house. They had grabbed my father, and dragged him away. Such raids, kidnapping men to crew the ships in Bristol port, were not uncommon.

"It all happened so sudden, like," Mrs Willerby explained. "There were no time for honest men to band together to stop 'em."

"Not that we'd've stood much chance, any road," added Gabriel Tunn, the sexton. "They was all scars and battle marks – 'sperienced fighters."

"Especially their captain," added Mrs Willerby. "Never seen such an evil-lookin' villain in all my days! One of his ears was cut right off – all he had was a blood-red hole goin' right into his head!"

Then I knew. It was Luggole Spain. The one-eared pirate had returned and carried off the only man alive who knew the golden secret. My father, my sole living relative, was in terrible danger and, young though I was, I had to try and save him.

Chapter 2

A Plan

When the truth of what had happened to my poor father sank in, I wept bitterly. The neighbours were very kind, and even offered to care for me. In my heart, though, I knew I could not accept, not while there was any chance of rescuing him.

So early the next morning I took the handful of gold coins father kept hidden beneath a floorboard in his workshop. I then wrapped a few spare clothes in a bundle, set my cap on my head and took the road down to Bristol. I had visited the famous seaport several times and knew my way through the winding streets to the docks. As I grew close, gulls screeched overhead. The quay was all bustle and business, loading and unloading, laughing and swearing, and the salty breeze was thick with the scent of fish, tobacco, tar and the distant sea.

There was no shortage of people to help me. The problem came when I started asking about Lambert Spain. The first man I approached spat into the gutter and looked away; the second gave me a slap round the head and told me to mind my own business. Only the third would talk.

"Well, mon petit ami," grinned Pierre Marchand, the plump cook of an ancient-looking French ship, *Le Roi d'Or*, "they say Monsieur Spain is bad man." He shrugged, his face creasing like pastry. "Maybe right, maybe wrong. I not know and not want to know."

He nodded towards a battered but seaworthy brigantine anchored some distance from the quayside. "They say that is his ship, the *Blue Parrot*. They also say it sail tonight for Port Royal, Jamaica." He shrugged again. "Maybe right, maybe wrong. I not know and not want to know."

I thanked Pierre for the information and stared across the choppy waters to where the blue-painted vessel rode at anchor. Men were busy on deck with sails and coils of rope. A rowing boat came out from the shore with what looked like barrels of stores. The chubby little Frenchman was almost certainly right – the *Blue Parrot*, with my father on board, was making ready to sail to the Caribbean.

Somehow, anyhow, I had to go there too. As I had nobody else to turn to, I told the cheery Frenchman how my father had been kidnapped and that I suspected he had been taken on board Spain's ship. Pierre chuckled, called me "mon brave" and offered to help.

That afternoon, sitting in the bar of the King's Head, we talked over what I could do. It was strange chatting to a Frenchman, seeing as we had been at war with France for so long. But now, in the spring of 1717, we had been at peace for four years, and Pierre was as kind and friendly a fellow as one could hope to meet.

"I'm going to try and sneak on board the *Blue Parrot* 'afore she sails," I suggested bravely. "Then I could hide away and help father escape when we get to Jamaica. Will you help me?"

Pierre looked at me and smiled. "Crazy! Do you want to die?"

"It could work," I insisted. "At least I'd be with father."

"Oui, it could work. But it could not. It's a very big risk, Arden. Are you sure you want to take it?"

Chapter 3

Discovery!

I couldn't have done it without Pierre. He was one of the best friends I ever had, poor man. Even now, years later, it still brings tears to my eyes when I think what they did to him.

But that dark episode lay ahead. I was still at Bristol docks, planning how to rescue my father from the *Blue Parrot*.

When I told Pierre that I was determined to sneak on board the pirate's ship and free my father, the kind-hearted cook called me a fool and an idiot. He called me much worse things, too, but in French, so I didn't understand.

He was too good a fellow to be grumpy for long, though, and he soon calmed down and said with a shrug, "Well, if you are determined to risk the life, I must be helping you."

* * *

First came the barrel, big enough for me to hide in but not so large that it couldn't be carried easily. Having shaken Pierre warmly by the hand, I lowered myself down into the sherry-smelling interior. My friend nailed the top down lightly so I'd be able to push it open when I was safely in the hold of the *Blue Parrot*. He then heaved the barrel –

with me jammed inside – on to a rowing boat and set off round the harbour.

"Biscuits," he cried. "Best ship's biscuits, going cheaps!" It was getting dark by the time he reached the *Blue Parrot*, and he called up to the cook that he could have the whole barrel full for just two shillings.

After five minutes of haggling and swearing, I felt the barrel being hauled up onto the deck. When it came to a standstill, I was still nervous, of course, and battered and bruised. But I had made it! I was on board the same ship as my kidnapped father.

I braced myself for the next stage of my journey: being lowered into the hold among the rest of the ship's stores. But no! To my horror, nothing further happened. The barrel, with me crammed inside it, remained on the deck.

* * *

Can you imagine my terror? The barrel must have been left there so the crew could help themselves when they felt hungry. That would mean opening the lid in broad daylight. Probably the very next morning. What's worse, I heard Luggole post a crew member on watch right next to where I was imprisoned, so there was no chance of escape.

I passed a sleepless night listening to his snores and racking my brains for something to do, something to say when the barrel was opened. If I failed, then, as Pierre had said, "You are dead, Arden – Pouf! Au revoir!"

* * *

When the first light of dawn showed through a crack in the lid of my prison, I heard the ship coming to life. Bare feet pattered on the wooden deck, gruff voices grumbled and a harsh command told someone to "secure that biscuit barrel to the mast!"

Then came the sound of the anchor being raised, followed by the flapping of the sails and creaking of the rigging. A few moments later, the *Blue Parrot* was under way. At first, all was well, but as the vessel left the shelter of the estuary and headed out into the Bristol Channel, the gentle swaying turned to a hideous rocking and pitching. My stomach churned. I was going to be sick…I clamped my hand over my mouth…I was going to be…Ugh!

Seconds later, one of the crew was levering off the barrel top with a knife. "Queer soundin' biscuits!" he muttered.

I gulped in the fresh sea air and blinked as bright daylight flooded in. A face appeared. Unshaven and broken-toothed, it stared for a moment, then vanished.

"Well I'll be keel-hauled!" a voice cried. "Come here, shipmates! Catch a look at what the cook's served up!"

Slowly, carefully, I raised my head and shoulders clear of the barrel and looked around. Above were billowing sails, below the swaying deck and the blue-grey expanse of the sea. But I didn't focus on these.

Gathered around me, grinning like fiends from hell, was a circle of the most cruel- and evil-looking men I had ever seen. One I recognized immediately. Of medium height, he was dressed in a long scarlet coat, frayed at the edges. No hat adorned his head and his long black hair was tied back behind the ears in a tarry pigtail.

Ears? No, not two ears but one. Where the left had been was now just a livid red scar around a dark hole. I was face to face with Lambert 'Luggole' Spain.

The captain's eyes narrowed. "Stowaways," he growled, "is thrown to the fishes."

I swallowed and began my speech. "Are you Cap'n Spain, sir? 'Cos if you be, then I have come here to serve you. I'm Tom Penfold, sir, and you are my hero."

Luggole snorted, but I could see that my flattery was having some effect. I went on to explain that for a long time it had been my greatest wish to sail with him and his famous crew. I wanted adventure, I wanted gold, and I had run away from home and smuggled myself on board to follow my dream.

"So, sir," I finished, climbing out of the barrel and kneeling before him, "throw me to the fishes if you will. But if you do, you will lose the most loyal servant and crew member you ever 'ad."

To my immense relief, it worked. After a brief discussion with Ebenezer Dag, the first mate, Luggole agreed to give me a trial as cabin boy. "But you put a foot out of place, boy, and you'll be joining our prisoner below. Or worse," he snarled, pointing to the cold, heaving ocean.

Chapter 4

'Traitor Tregorey'

'The prisoner below' Spain had said. Now I knew father was definitely being held on the *Blue Parrot*, I planned my next moves very carefully. I did my work – cleaning, fetching and carrying – as well as anyone could have expected. Luckily, my seasickness did not last long – I must have some of father's sailor's blood in my veins. Even when we ran into a storm in mid-Atlantic and giant waves broke over the bows, I felt as at home on deck as I had back on dry land.

Before long, thanks to my cheery manner and willingness to help, I was everyone's friend. Everyone except Ebenezer Dag, that is. Tall and lean, with colourless, close-set eyes that seemed to follow me wherever I went, he sent shivers down my spine. I didn't trust him one peck – and before long my suspicion was proved right.

Bit by bit I learned from the crew that my father – 'Traitor Tregorey' they called him – had once stolen a trunk stuffed with jewels that belonged to the captain. More than a dozen years later, the pirate had found where Tregorey was living, seized him and was now taking him to Hispaniola to show them where he had buried the treasure.

All that talk of Jamaica, I realized, had been a trick to throw pursuers off the scent. "And when the treacherous devil's shown you the place?" I asked, acting as innocent as I could. "What then?"

The pirates laughed. After that, they agreed, the captain would kill the traitor, sure as gulls was gulls.

Realizing the peril of father's situation, I determined to get to see him as soon as possible. I knew where he was – in a small cabin below the captain's – but I was not allowed anywhere near that part of the ship. All I could do was wait…and hope.

* * *

My chance came right at the end of the voyage. By now we were in the tropics and the air had grown hot and humid. All the crew, except the captain and the first mate, went about stripped to the waist. At last, late one afternoon, the green hills of Hispaniola came into sight. The moment the cry "Land ahoy!" echoed through the thick, moist air, the crew rushed on deck to take a look. Seizing my opportunity, I sneaked through the doorway below the poop deck, down the stairs and pushed at the door of the cabin in which my father was held. To my relief, it was not locked. I swung it open, stepped inside and closed the door behind me.

At first I did not recognize him. The last time I had seen my father he was a strong, sturdy man with a brown, clean-shaven face. The figure before me, chained to a bench, was thin and pale, with long hair and a tangled grey beard. Only his clear, honest blue eyes had not changed.

"Father!" I cried, rushing towards him. "What have they done to you?" I fell before him, tugging at the rusty chains.

Even as I did so, I heard a noise behind me. Someone was coming down the stairway towards the cabin. Grabbing a heavy brass candlestick from a small table near the window, I darted behind the high-backed chair beside it. It was not much of a hiding place, but it had to do.

Seconds later, the door opened and Ebenezer Dag slid into the room. "Well, Traitor," he sneered, kicking at father's chains, "where's your littl' visitor, then?"

Chapter 5

Merciless!

I shan't pretend – I was terrified.
There I was, clutching a candlestick
and hiding behind a chair in a tiny
cabin on board a pirate ship. Only a
few feet away stood the looming
figure of Ebenezer Dag, one of the
most villainous of all the pirate crew.
Before him, chained to a bench, sat
my poor father.

"You hear me, Traitor Tregorey?"
Dag snarled. "Where's that brat of
a son of yours?"

No wonder Dag had been watching me so closely! More sharp-eyed than the rest of the crew, he had realized who I was.

"Thought so!" he went on. "How sweet! The traitor's son come to rescue his poor daddy! Ha! We'll see about that!"

"I, I don't know what you's a-talkin' of, Ebenezer my old shipmate," father answered, trying to sound innocent. His voice, normally strong, was thin and weak like an old man's.

"Liar! An' don't you 'shipmate' me, you snivellin' traitor!"

There was a sickening crack, followed by a muffled cry. "Tell me where that rat-faced son of yours is, Tregorey, or you'll be feeling my fist a lot harder."

I could take no more. Clutching the candlestick firmly in my right hand, I stood up and faced Dag. I was glad of the chair – it hid my quivering knees.

"I'm here… Dag," I said. "And I'm not afraid of you!"

As the pirate lurched towards me, I flung the candlestick at him with all my strength. It missed his head by a good two feet and smashed against the bench to which father was chained.

With a malicious grin, Dag drew his knife and advanced towards me. Panic gave me added strength. With a heave, I thrust the chair at him and darted to the left. The pirate shoved the chair aside as if it were made of feathers. I was trapped.

Dag lifted his wicked blade and took another a step forward. He was now just three feet away, within striking distance. The knife rose high in the air, the blade glinting like a jewel in the tropical sun streaming in through the window. I closed my eyes….

Crash! Something heavy fell to the wooden floor. I opened my eyes to see the crumpled form of Ebenezer Dag fall to his knees and then pitch forward. Father had picked up the heavy brass candlestick and hurled it with deadly accuracy at the pirate's head. The blow had knocked him out cold!

"Well thrown, father!" I cried, rushing to his side. "You've saved us!"

He soon convinced me how wrong I was. We were anything but safe and needed a plan of escape – now.

First, I took from Dag's pocket the keys to the padlocks that fastened father's chains, and set him free. Rubbing his chafed ankles, he looked down at the pirate's prone body. "He knows everything," he muttered. "Maybe we should finish him off."

I shook my head. "No, father. That ain't right. We'd be no better than pirates ourselves if we did that."

Father nodded. The best plan, we decided, was to throw Dag out of the window into the sea. It was easier said than done. Although not a heavy man, he was an awkward, gangly shape and it took us three attempts to get him through the narrow opening. Finally, while father held him by the shoulders, I steered his feet out over the ocean.

To my dismay, the pirate came round just as we were heaving him clear. He stared wildly about him, made a strange gurgling sound, and then vanished. Leaning out to see what happened, I saw him hit the water with a splash and watch miserably as the *Blue Parrot* slipped rapidly away from him. When it was clear that his colleagues couldn't hear his cries for help above the noise of the sea, he struck out for the shore of Hispaniola barely half a mile away.

That, I hoped, would be the last we would ever see of Ebenezer Dag.

As father was too weak to attempt his own escape, he locked himself back in his chains and hid the key in his breeches.

"Now you go back to Luggole," he commanded, "and say you saw Dag fall into the drink. Say 'e was drunk. When we gets to land, I can unlock myself, sneak out and join you. Then I'll tell you my secret!"

* * *

Back on deck, just as I was approaching the crew with my story of how Dag had fallen overboard, a cannon boomed somewhere astern. The pirates were as startled as I was, and we all hurried to the gunwale to see where the noise had come from.

A vessel was on our tail. Not just any vessel, either. It was the 28-gun frigate HMS *Merciless*, commanded by Joshua Gilbert. One of the ablest but harshest captains in the entire Royal Navy, Gilbert was on anti-piracy patrol in the Caribbean.

The *Blue Parrot* didn't stand a chance.

Luggole was not one to give up easily, though. The instant he realized what was happening, he ordered the crew to hoist as much sail as the *Parrot* could bear. "We'll give the scurvy scum a run for their money!" he yelled, running up to the poop deck and grabbing the helm.

It was pointless. The *Merciless* closed on us with every breath of wind. When a second cannon shot whistled into the rigging above Luggole's head, tearing away the sail, he realized it was time to change tactic.

Summoning his crew, he outlined his thinking. "I know Gilbert and his *Merciless*," he cried. "Huntin' me for years, an' now they think they've got me. But no navy toff's goin' to get the better of old Spain! So long as we's got breath, we've got a chance, eh?"

The crew growled their agreement.

"This is how it'll play out," Luggole went on. "We'll let 'em take us – but see that Tregorey is taken too." He paused for a moment, looking round with a ferocious eye. "Tell 'em he's one of the crew and we clapped 'im in irons for disobeying orders. He can protest, but they won't believe him!"

A wave of vulgar laughter rippled around the deck. Spain raised his hand for silence. "Then, when we's taken back to Port Royal, Jamaica, I'll see ye set free and we'll go find the treasure what the traitor stole off of us. I've friends in high places there as owes me. Trust me, lads?"

"Aye! Aye!" cheered the crew.

I was the only one not smiling. Just when I thought I had succeeded in setting father free, fate had dealt us a cruel blow. Now we would both be arrested for piracy. And the punishment for that crime was hanging by the neck until dead.

Chapter 6

Imprisoned!

Events did not turn out quite as Luggole had predicted. The *Blue Parrot*'s sails were lowered, the *Merciless* came alongside and we surrendered without a fight. Captain Gilbert, a short, bright-eyed man with a fox-coloured beard, grinned in delight as the pirate crew handed over their weapons. Scowling with fury, they were led across a gangplank into the dark hold of the warship.

When father was found and started explaining who he was, Gilbert did not believe a word. Father was not helped by the pirates calling him 'Billy' and 'shipmate'. "Besides," Gilbert added, staring closely at father, "I know the name 'Tregorey'. Rings a bell. Something to do with stealing treasure from….Who was it? Yes, the McKinleys. That was the name. Years ago."

"I can explain…" father began, screwing his hands together in wretchedness.

"Indeed?" cut in Gilbert. "You certainly have a lot of explaining to do. Take him away!"

I was mystified. Were these people, the McKinleys, part of father's secret? I wondered whether I should tell the captain my story, but decided against it. It was too fantastical. Besides, hadn't I joined the *Blue Parrot* of my own free will? Worse, if the brigands learned the truth, goodness knows what they would do to me in the darkness of the hold.

Thus far, Luggole's plan had worked. When he himself appeared before Gilbert, however, it quickly fell apart.

"We meet at last, Spain," crowed the captain. "Pity you surrendered. I would have enjoyed sending you and your crew to the bottom. Now it'll just be the noose."

Luggole scowled back at him. "Noose, eh? A good English jury has to find me guilty first, Gilbert."

The captain laughed. "English jury? Not for you, Spain. We're taking you to Port-au-Prince in Hispaniola, not Port Royal, Jamaica."

The blood drained from Luggole's face. "Port-au-Prince? That's French."

"Precisely," replied Gilbert, his eyes narrowing. "You see, the French also want you for piracy. They don't believe in juries. The verdict – guilty or innocent – is given by a magistrate. In Port-au-Prince he happens to be a friend of mine, Bertrand Doat. I think Monsieur Doat can be guaranteed to deliver a guilty verdict."

* * *

Inside the dank and evil-smelling hold of the *Merciless*, the pirates sat around in groups, cursing and swearing. I kept to myself, overcome with misery. Father, sitting a few yards away, did his best to cheer me up by winking when no one was looking. To be honest, it didn't help much.

Hours later, exhausted and more unhappy than ever, I fell asleep. It was still dark when I was woken by someone tugging at my sleeve. It was father. We grasped each other warmly and, taking care no one heard or saw us, whispered our stories to each other.

Mine was soon told. After thanking me and calling me "the bravest lad in all England", it was father's turn. Years ago, he said, the wealthy Mr and Mrs McKinley employed him to guard their fortune on a voyage between Carolina and England. The vessel was attacked by Luggole.

"What happened next," he went on, looking round to make sure we were not overheard, "was what fetched me into this mess. Just like you, Arden, I pretended to join with the pirate crew. A week later, I stuffed the McKinley treasure into a sea chest and escaped with it. My plan was to keep it safe then give it back to its rightful owners.

"But knowing as Luggole would come after me, I buried the chest on Hispaniola for safe keeping. In case something happened to me, I drawed a map of where it lay and hid it 'neath the altar inside the church at Port-au-Prince. As far as I knows, the treasure and the map are both safe where I left 'em.

"Later, I heard that Luggole had left the McKinleys on a deserted island to perish. The evil man said it was a 'punishment' for losing 'his' treasure. Not only that, but he swore to find me and force me to tell 'im where that treasure was. I can't tell 'e what 'e said he'd do to make me talk.

"Best course, I decided, was to lie low. I came back to Bristol, set myself up as a cobbler and settled down with your dear mother. I was plannin' to return to the Caribbean one day, when you was older, to dig up the treasure and hand it over to the McKinley's only son.

"You know the rest, don't 'e? Luggole and his men tracked me down….

At this point, the man beside us stirred and father crept back to the other side of the hold. I finally understood what was going on. But what good would it do me, or father,

I wondered, if we were both to be hanged? There seemed no way out.

The following day the *Merciless* dropped anchor at Port-au-Prince, and we were rowed ashore. The town, surrounded by towering green mountains, was a sorry affair. Ramshackle wooden houses lined dirty streets in which dogs and filthy children played in the mud. The citizens stared at us open mouthed as we were led to a large, sombre-looking building some half a mile from the harbour.

It was the town prison. Once inside, we were searched and thrown, six at a time, into dingy, damp cells. From time to time, surly guards gave us hard black bread and water from a rusty can. Both were disgusting. For three days we sat in silence in the stifling tropical heat, staring at the beetles crawling across the floor and wondering what would become of us.

Then, on the morning of the fourth day, we were woken by yells echoing down the corridor outside. Something had happened. I put my ear to the door but could hear nothing but confused shouting. All became clear about half an hour later when one of the sailors from the *Merciless*, who was acting as a guard, came in with our breakfast.

"So what's all that caterwauling?" asked one of my cell mates, a skull-faced villain known as Slashing Sam.

The sailor guard looked at each of us in turn. "Well," he said cautiously, "I don't suppose as there's much 'arm in you knowing. Last night three of you felons got out. Some villain cut through the wall of their cell from the outside and they scarpered."

My brain raced. Help from outside? Then I realized…Ebenezer Dag. He must have made it to shore.

"Good on 'em," grunted Sam.

The guard spat in the dust at his feet. "Good? They won't get far. And when we find 'em, we've orders to shoot 'em on sight."

"If you find 'em," Sam smirked. "So who was they?"

I leaned forward, desperate to hear his reply.

"One of them was Spain." My heart beat furiously as I waited for what would follow. "I don't know the names of the other pair, but one of them was that scrawny fellow we found in irons – "

"Tregorey!" I blurted without thinking. "Bill Tregorey, my fath…."

Although I stopped before the word was out, it was too late. The guard gave me a strange look, turned on his heel and left the room. How could I have been so stupid? I put my head in my hands and cowered into a corner, covering my ears so I couldn't hear the questions Sam was firing at me.

A little while later, the cell door opened and the guard reappeared. Without a word, he grabbed me by the collar and hauled me into the corridor. To my surprise, he took me out of the front door of the prison to where Captain Gilbert sat at a table smoking a pipe in the shade of a spreading palm tree. He eyed me closely for a while.

"So you know Bill Tregorey?" he asked eventually. "Rather well, I hear."

I shrugged. Glancing nervously around, I noted that to my left the forest came almost up to the walls of the prison. Once under the cover of the tangled trees and creepers, it'd be nigh on impossible to find me.

Gilbert's voice interrupted my wild thoughts. "Maybe you have a good idea where Tregorey and Spain are headed, eh?"

"I d-don't know," I stuttered, thinking hard. Should I tell him about the map? If I did, they might get Spain before he found the treasure. But father might be killed. After all, the Captain seemed certain he was a pirate, and his men had orders to shoot the escaped prisoners on sight.

"Come on," snapped Gilbert. "You can do better than that, surely?"

Even now, I'm not sure why I did it. I suppose I was desperate, ready to do anything to help my father. He was all I had in the world.

Taking a sudden step forward, I shoved the sturdy teak table hard into Captain Gilbert's stomach. With a gasp of surprise, he toppled heavily backwards into the dirt.

Hearing the noise, the guard swung round and came bounding towards me. I grabbed a spare chair and flung it at his legs. As he sprawled headlong, I dashed round to where the Captain lay winded, seized the dagger from his side and sprinted for the forest.

I had a lead of a good fifteen paces over the guard by the time I reached the undergrowth. It was not enough. Thorns scratched my arms and face, creepers clawed at my legs. The further I penetrated, the nearer drew the crashing behind me.

My adult pursuer was able to push aside branches that I had to duck under or go round. After five minutes, the fifteen paces had become ten, then seven. The guard's angry yells became louder and louder.

Glancing ahead, I noticed the ground rising, gradually at first then quite steeply. Over the top of the ridge dangled long creepers, like tentacles. They were my only hope. I had to reach the summit first.

Scrambling, crawling, gasping for breath like a hunted animal, I dragged my way upwards. By the time I reached the top, the guard was almost upon me. I took a couple of steps back from the edge, grabbed a creeper and swung out over the incline.

My feet caught the guard square in the chest, knocking him clean off his feet. Panting, I watched as he tumbled over and over down the slope. At the bottom, arms outstretched as if he were yawning, he lay unconscious.

I had escaped.

Chapter 7

A Happy Reunion

I spent the rest of the morning climbing further and further into the hills. By the time I stopped for breath, the jungle was so dense and tangled that not even a fleet of sailors searching for a month could have found me.

I quenched my thirst at a fast-running stream and dined off the plentiful fruits and nuts growing all around. Then, having settled myself in the branches of a small rosewood tree for safety, I made my plan.

Luggole, Ebenezer Dag and Joseph Scallow, the man who had escaped with Luggole, would force father to say where he had buried the treasure. With him as their guide, they would then make for the place after dark. I had to get there too, as soon as possible after nightfall. Father didn't need the map, of course, but I did – that meant a visit to the church.

In the middle of the afternoon, I climbed to the top of the tallest tree I could find. Some three miles away, the small town lay spread out before me. The church was obvious. One of the few stone buildings, it stood about 500 yards inland from the quay. If I skirted to the east, I could reach it by passing along no more than a couple of streets.

* * *

There was no nightlife in Port-au-Prince. For whatever reason, as darkness fell, the citizens withdrew into their houses and closed the shutters. Maybe they were afraid of the ghosts of dead slaves and sailors that were rumoured to haunt the island after sundown?

Through the deserted streets I went, stalking from shadow to shadow until I arrived at the heavy wooden door of the church. As it creaked open on its rusty hinges, the sweet smell of incense drifted out into the tropical night. I tiptoed inside and closed the door. An eerie silence greeted me.

Carefully, step by step, I made my way down the aisle towards the altar. Halfway down, I paused. I had an uncomfortable feeling that someone was watching me. I turned. At the back of the church, to the left of the door, a figure was on its knees praying.

Horrified, I sprinted back down the aisle. The figure, bulky though it was, was too quick for me. A large hand grabbed my arm and spun me round. To my astonishment I found myself staring into the face of a friend.

"Pierre!" I gasped. "What are you…?"

"I am asking the same question, mon ami!" grinned the chubby French cook of *Le Roi d'Or*. "I was in 'ere to pray for you. I am hearing you are in big trouble, yes?"

Dear Pierre! First he had helped me board the *Blue Parrot* in Bristol and now, on the other side of the Atlantic, he was still trying to help me.

Our stories were quickly told. On reaching Hispaniola safely, Pierre had learned all about Luggole Spain and HMS *Merciless*. He had been on his way to the prison to explain my innocence when he heard of my escape. "Then I realize you are in *very* big trouble, petit Arden," he frowned.

Hearing my tale and realizing how father was in even deeper trouble than me, he immediately agreed to assist me. First, we had to find the map. Pierre advanced to the altar and carefully pulled aside the white cloth covering it. By the light of his lantern, he began his examination.

"Impossible!" he grunted, moving to the other side. When he had made a complete tour, he invited me to join him. Together we crawled right round again and came to the same conclusion. The altar was made of one block of solid marble and must have weighed at least a ton.

There was no way my father could have hidden anything beneath it.

Pierre rose heavily to his feet. "Well, there is only two possibilities, mon ami," he said with a sigh. "Either there is no map and your dear father was mistaking or forgetting, or somebody has taken it."

"I don't think either's possible, Pierre," I replied, sitting down on the altar steps. "Father told me clear as glass where it was. He put it beneath a stone tile right under the altar. But not even a mouse would go creepin' in there!"

Even as I spoke, I was aware of a ghostly shape coming towards us out of the shadows. "That is where you is going wrong, my friend," said a smooth, almost treacly voice with a thick Spanish accent.

Chapter 8

The Pit

The shadow drew closer. "Who are you?" I demanded, standing up and reaching for my dagger. Out of the corner of my eye I saw Pierre draw his pistol.

As the figure stepped into the light of our lantern we made out a clean-shaven man of medium height dressed in the long, black robes of a Roman Catholic priest.

"My name is Father Benedicto," he explained in the same cool, smooth tone. "I am priest here in Hôpital –

you is calling it Port-au-Prince. Welcome in my church, my dear friends."

Pierre replaced his pistol in its holster and came forward, beaming. "Father! I am so 'appy to see you. I am attending mass in zis church two times, and you are the priest."

Father Benedicto nodded. "Yes, I know your face, my son."

Far in the back of my mind, a tiny alarm bell rang. There was something about this priest – this holy man – that made me feel uncomfortable. He was just too gracious, too good to be true. And the voice…Its humbleness, its sweetness was so oily.

"Excuse me, father," I interrupted, "but we are here on a mission. We need your help."

The priest turned his pale face in my direction and fixed me with eyes that gleamed yellow in the candlelight. "Of course I help you, child. I know why you is here." He put his hand inside his robe and pulled out a roll of parchment. "This is what you is seeking, I believe? Take it, please."

I took the roll and unwound it as Pierre brought the lantern closer. It was the map! It clearly showed Port-au-Prince, the ocean, the hills a short distance to the south – and in those hills an X in bold, black ink.

"This is it, Pierre!" I cried, clapping my friend on the shoulder. "And thank you father," I added, turning to the priest.

He smiled calmly, so calmly. When I asked him how he had come by the map, he said that a few years back an earthquake had shaken the island. The church had not been badly damaged, but the altar had cracked and needed to be replaced. During the work, he noticed a loose tile, and beneath it….

He had broken the seal and opened the scroll, he explained, but it was of no interest to him. "I no understand. Some mark in the mountain. You know what is it?"

He looked at me carefully, his yellow eyes narrowing slightly. No, I did not want this man to know the truth. I couldn't explain why, but I didn't trust him. "Er, yes. I can explain it to you," I began, making it up as I went along. "My father made it."

I said my father was a sailor – that part was true anyway – and visiting Hispaniola some years back, he had lost a precious crucifix from round his neck. It was a family heirloom, given him by his mother. He searched where he thought it had fallen but, as his ship was leaving immediately, he had to stop before he found it.

Hoping to return one day, he made a map of where he believed the crucifix lay and hid it under the altar. Sadly, he died of the plague the following year – but not before he had told me his story.

"So you can imagine my sorrow," I concluded, "when I found the map had gone."

"And you, my child, can imagine my pleasure when I give you key to your father's treasure, eh?"

My heart jumped. Had he said "father's treasure" to test me? Had his lips twitched slightly when he saw my reaction to the phrase?

I wiped the thought from my mind. There was no time for such doubts. Father was in desperate danger and we had to find him as quickly as possible. The map showed us the way.

Thanking Father Benedicto warmly for his help, we left the church and set out into the hot, sticky tropical night.

* * *

Our journey was like something from one of those fairy tales we had been told at the dame school back in Bedminster. The moon hung above us like a gigantic silver coin. Treasure lighting us the way to treasure, I thought. The thick air was alive with strange hoots, barks and howls. Beneath our feet, unseen creatures slithered into the undergrowth at our approach.

We made our way out of the town unseen. Just past the last shack, we picked up a dirt track that wound through a handful of muddy fields before it entered the jungle. Every now and again, we paused and Pierre held his lantern up to the map to check we were headed in the right direction.

Behind us, the ocean gleamed like mercury beyond the grave black shape of the town. Before us loomed the tree-covered hills. After the first rise, the map showed a shallow ravine with a sandy bottom. At its centre, twenty paces to the west of a large boulder, lay the McKinley treasure.

Needing to keep a sharp ear out for suspicious sounds, we didn't talk much. I prayed we might hear Luggole and his accomplices talking rather than father's cries as they demanded to know where the chest lay buried. I also kept watch on the path behind us. What if I were right and the priest was not to be trusted? Maybe he had sent a search party on our trail already? And what if he had lied about not exploring what lay beneath the X on the map?

So many things could go wrong, I told myself, there was no point in worrying. All I had to do now was reach father before it was too late.

* * *

The map, though only roughly
sketched, was remarkably accurate.
After the track had wound up the first
hill for about half a mile, it suddenly
turned to the right. The reason was
obvious. Ahead the trees came to an
abrupt halt and the ground fell steeply
away into a ravine about fifty feet deep.

Two voices, one loud and rasping, the
other quiet and anxious, floated up into
the still night air. I recognized them
both instantly.

Pierre and I glanced at each other and
crept to the top of the slope. Lit by the
brilliant moonlight, the scene below
was as clear as if it had been daylight.
Luggole stood, pistol in hand, staring
down into a large hole. Father, just his

head and shoulders visible, was in the pit, digging. The other two pirates were nowhere to be seen.

"I have your word, Spain?" father asked, resting on his spade for a moment. "You promise on the Holy Bible you won't do Arden no harm after this treasure's found?"

Luggole spat in the sand. "You have my word, Tregorey. Swear on my father's grave – 'cept he ain't got no grave. He drowned! Ha! ha!"

The cruelty of the laugh made me shiver, despite the warmth of the night.

"Anycourse," Luggole continued, "'e's safe and you's safe only when you finds that chest. You bin diggin' a long time, Tregorey, and ain't found nothin' yet."

"It's here Spain, I promise," replied father, thrusting his spade into the sand again. A loud clang brought Luggole nearer to the edge of the pit.

"Wassit?" he demanded. "What yer found down there?" He cocked his pistol. "If it's treasure, Tregory, you done your job. Thankee!"

I grabbed Pierre's arm. He was going to kill father! Now the treasure was uncovered, Luggole had no further use for him.

I was on the point of shouting out when I heard a loud double click behind me. I spun round. Barely two feet away, a brace of pistols was pointing straight at my heart.

Chapter 9

Betrayed!

We should have known that Luggole Spain was too clever to leave himself unguarded. It was our fault – and now our very lives were in danger.

Ebenezer Dag and Joseph Scallow had been keeping watch while Luggole forced my father to dig for the treasure chest he had buried all those years ago. Pierre and I were so worried about what Luggole would do if father couldn't find the chest, we didn't hear the two pirates sneak up behind us.

Now we were caught like hares in a snare.

Keeping his pistols trained on me, Dag called out: "Oi! Captain! Guess who's turned up?"

Luggole's rasping voice floated up from the bottom of the ravine. "Let me think…Hey! Not Traitor Tregorey's son by any chance?"

"Aye-aye, sir!" Dag replied in mock naval tones. "And the Frenchie. The one as sold us that barrel back in Bristol." A pair of iron pistols jabbed painfully into my ribs. "Bringin' 'em down now, Cap'n!"

As Dag kept me covered, Scallow searched my clothing and removed the knife I had stolen from Captain Gilbert. Then, with guns still on me every step of the way, I climbed slowly to the bottom of the moonlit ravine. To my right, Joseph Scallow was forcing Pierre to the same destination. Poor man! I thought. He was probably going to be killed just for helping a friend.

We were halted on the edge of the pit. I glanced down at father, searching for a glint of hope in his tired eyes. There was nothing.

Luggole sauntered over and stood before me. "So what's this then?" he asked, snatching the map from my hand and unfolding it. The pirates had already forced father to tell them where the treasure was, so I thought the map didn't matter any more. It only told them what they already knew.

As it turned out, that's where I was wrong.

Holding the parchment up to the moonlight, Luggole looked at it carefully then glanced around the ravine. "Aye," he muttered eventually, "'tis same place 'ere as on the map. So you weren't lyin', Bill Tregorey."

"I told you so, Spain," father began. "This is where I buried–"

The villain cut him short with an oath and ordered him to continue digging. "Afore we was in'errupted," he growled, "I heard you strike somethin'. Couldn't be that chest, now, could it?"

I quietly prayed it wasn't. The moment father uncovered the treasure chest, we would be of no use to the pirates and they might well shoot us. But father did not uncover the chest. The object his spadc had hit against was simply a stone. After digging for a further ten minutes, he looked up in desperation.

"Not 'ere, Spain," he panted. "Promise. I buried it no more 'n' three feet deep. Recall it as clear as water. I'm now down six foot. It's gone, I tell 'ee. Someone's been an' taken it."

Luggole let fall a mighty curse. His awful face, half in shadow, twisted like a ship in a storm and I feared he was going to kill father there and then. But the tempest passed as swiftly as it had arisen and no shot was fired. Instead, he turned and asked me when father had handed over the map.

"He never," I answered, deciding truth was the best option. "He told me he hid it in the church."

The villainous pirate's watery blue eyes narrowed. "So that's 'ow you came by it then?"

As briefly as I could, I explained what had taken place inside the church: how Father Benedicto had found the map and given it to me. Even as I was telling the story, I realized what must have happened.

The priest had found the map, dug up the treasure and hidden it. No wonder he had looked so guilty! He had almost certainly told the authorities where we were, too. Once we were out of the way, the treasure would be his to use as he saw fit. No doubt a band of French soldiers was headed in our direction even now.

I glanced at Luggole. The expression on his pitted face told that he had been thinking along exactly the same lines as me.

"That priest," he muttered. "He's double-crossed us! Just wait till I gets my 'ands on 'im!"

As time was short, Luggole wanted to shoot father, Pierre and me, and bury our bodies in the pit. Surprisingly, it was Ebenezer Dag
who saved us. It would take a good half hour to bury the bodies, he argued. Besides, shooting us would waste valuable ammunition and the noise of the guns would tell anyone for miles around where we were.

No, he concluded, the best plan was to gag and bind us. By the time we were found, the pirates and the treasure would be over the horizon.

Luggole gave him a strange look, as if he were not so sure he agreed with everything Dag had said. But he went along with the plan. The pirates bound us hand and foot with ropes they had brought, and gagged our mouths with strips torn from our own shirts. That done, they pushed Pierre and me into the pit beside father and left.

Chapter 10

The Chase

The events that followed were the most important of my short life. In just two brief hours, I experienced tragedy and triumph, and bade farewell to childhood for ever. To this day, I still dream of that extraordinary night.

Freeing ourselves was easier than we had thought possible. I made the first move, wriggling over to the spade and rubbing the rope that bound my wrists against its sharp blade. Within ten minutes I was free. In another ten,

I had undone the ropes holding father and Pierre and we had taken off our gags.

Getting all three of us out of the pit proved more difficult. I went first, standing on a step father made with his hands. He followed, helped by me from above and Pierre from below. Freeing the Frenchman was rather harder. He was too heavy for us to pull, so father and I had to go back down into the hole and push him. Desperate though our situation was, the bizarre operation made us all chuckle.

When father and I had scrambled out of the pit to join Pierre, we set off back the way we had come. Every now and again we stopped and listened for a patrol coming out to find us. Not a sound.

We were well into the small hours of the night by the time we reached Port-au-Prince, and the town was deathly quiet. A dog opened one sleepy eye as we crept by, but closed it again when it realized we were no threat to him or to his household.

To our surprise, we found the church door already open. Flickering candlelight played on the stone step outside. Someone inside, we realized, was still awake.

Father went first, slipping through the doorway before darting into the shadowy aisle to his left. We followed, me first and Pierre bringing up the rear. As our eyes became accustomed to the gloom, we noticed a figure lying beside the altar. It was Father Benedicto.

The priest was in a bad way. We knelt beside him and did what we could to sooth his cuts and bruises. He confessed that, yes, he had indeed dug up the treasure. He had put it in a safe place in the crypt of this very church. He had planned to sell the jewels and give the money to the poor of the town. How he now regretted not telling the authorities what he knew!

A short while earlier, he explained, he had been woken by a noise inside the church. Hurrying from his house next door, he had found Luggole and his accomplices ransacking the place of worship. They grabbed him, beat him up and forced him to tell them where he had put the treasure chest.

"And where are these pirates now?" father asked, glancing anxiously around.

He was answered by two muffled pistol shots echoing from the crypt beneath us. A minute later, a door opened and Luggole emerged to our right. In his arms was a brass-bound chest. From his gnarled fingers a lantern swung slowly back and forth.

Glancing to where he had left the priest, the pirate saw us at once. Dropping the chest, he drew a brace of pistols from the deep pockets of his tattered red coat. "Well I'll be keelhauled!" he said. "If it's not them Tregoreys and their foreign friend again!"

A cruel smile cracked his thin lips. "Come to think of it, I'm glad you've come along. I could do with a bit of an 'and."

It was soon horribly clear what he meant. Threatening to kill me if we made a false move, he forced Pierre to pick up the chest. He then said with a fearful oath that he and his prisoner were leaving and if anyone came after them or raised the alarm, 'the Frenchie' would die. With those words, and with Pierre walking a foot in front of him carrying the chest, the evil scoundrel left the church.

* * *

Father and I stared at each other. What now? The McKinley treasure was lost, Luggole had got away and my loyal friend was in terrible danger. In despair, I took a candle from the altar and went to see what the shooting in the crypt had been about.

I suspected foul deeds – and I was right. Once he had located the treasure chest, Luggole had decided to share it with no one. Dag and Scallow, his own shipmates, had each received a bullet from his pistols. Both lay on the floor, seriously wounded.

Fury swelled up inside me. What sort of monster was this who betrayed and shot his own men? He could not be allowed to get away with it. He must not!

I grabbed a pistol from each of the wounded pirates and ran back to my father. "I'm sorry father," I said, my voice husky with emotion, "but I must go."

"Go?"

"After Luggole Spain," I explained. "You stay here and look after father

Benedicto. You'll find two more unfortunate villains in the crypt, too."

I held tight to father's hand for a second or two before turning away. With a lump in my throat, I stumbled out into the night. The darkness was not the only reason I could not see clearly for a minute or two.

Luggole had reached the harbour by the time I caught up with him. The moon had gone down and warm fingers of dawn were colouring the distant horizon. A stiff breeze was rattling the rigging on the boats. I hid behind a pile of gravel used for ships' ballast and watched. The pirate forced Pierre, still carrying the chest, to step down into a cutter moored alongside the jetty. Moments later, the boat was cast off.

Luggole was a skilful sailor. I watched in reluctant admiration as, keeping his pistol still trained on Pierre, he raised a sail and soon had the cutter skimming out towards the distant sea.

I had failed. As there was no need to keep hidden any longer, I walked down to the edge of the quay and watched the small boat getting further and further from the shore. The first scarlet rays of sunrise glinted over the water, forcing me to screw up my eyes against the glare.

Luggole had moved towards Pierre and seemed to be speaking to him. The Frenchman stood up, holding out his arms to balance. His captor suddenly lunged forward, swung his pistol and knocked Pierre over the side of the boat into the sea. Something my friend had once said to me came flooding back. "Oui, it is strange, mon ami. I have been a sailor all my life, but I cannot swim."

Cannot swim? He was going to drown!

I sprinted down the quay looking for a suitable boat. This would do: a small but speedy-looking lighter. I jumped aboard, unfastened her and pushed off. Seconds later I had the sail up and was racing out towards the spot where Pierre had disappeared.

I was too late. When I reached the place and looked desperately around, there was nothing to be seen but the dark purple of the ocean. Pierre, who had loved me like a second father, was gone for ever. A single thought gripped my mind: this cruel death must not go unpunished.

My boat was quicker than Luggole's. The sail hummed and small waves slapped against the bow as I urged her forward. Minute by minute, furlong by furlong, I gained on my adversary. Quite what I would do when I caught up with him, I was not sure. In the end, fortune decided for me.

In vain, Luggole weaved from side to side to throw me off. I was not giving up now. When there were no more than ten yards between us, the villain drew his pistols. The first shot whistled by my left ear and splashed harmlessly into the sea astern. The second passed through the sail above my head.

Two pistols, two shots. As I suspected, he needed to reload. Capable sailor though he was, even Luggole could not handle a small boat and load a pistol at the same time. He took his hand off the tiller for a second, a gust of wind caught the sail – and she was over. The pirate and the brass-bound chest toppled into the sea.

Only one of them reappeared.

* * *

I secured a line to Luggole's upturned boat and, with the dripping pirate clinging to its bottom, headed back to the harbour. By the time I reached the quayside, quite a reception committee had gathered. Father was there, standing beside Captain Gilbert and several of the crew of the *Merciless*. The captain obviously knew the truth now because it was he who called for three hearty cheers as I stepped ashore.

The last time I saw Luggole Spain he was being escorted back to prison with chains firmly attached round both ankles. There was little chance of his escaping this time. As far as I know, the McKinley jewels on which he had set his wicked heart still lie in that brass-bound chest at the bottom of the sea.

* * *

The well-meaning Father Benedicto is now a bishop. Though the pirates had failed to make themselves rich, father and I were more fortunate. From Captain Gilbert we learned that a handsome reward had been offered for the capture of Lambert Spain, dead or alive. "It's all yours, Arden Tregorey," he beamed. "And you thoroughly deserve it, too!"

We collected the money on our return to Bristol. It turned out to be even more than we thought, enough for me to resume my studies and father to buy a small inn. We named it the 'Friendly Frenchman' in memory of Pierre. So in the end, though we had been through a hard and painful adventure, things did not turn out so badly after all, did they?

THE END

FICTION EXPRESS

THE READERS TAKE CONTROL!

Have you ever wanted to change the course of a plot, change a character's destiny, tell an author what to write next?

Well, now you can!

'The Pirate's Secret' was originally written for the award-winning interactive e-book website Fiction Express.

Fiction Express e-books are published in gripping weekly episodes. At the end of each episode, readers are given voting options to decide where the plot goes next. They vote online and the winning vote is then conveyed to the author who writes the next episode, in real time, according to the readers' most popular choice.

www.fictionexpress.co.uk

WINNER
Education Resources
Award for Innovation

FICTI●N EXPRESS

TALK TO THE AUTHORS

The Fiction Express website features a blog where readers can interact with the authors while they are writing. An exciting and unique opportunity!

FANTASTIC TEACHER RESOURCES

Each weekly Fiction Express episode comes with a PDF of teacher resources packed with ideas to extend the text.

"The teaching resources are fab and easily fill a whole week of literacy lessons!"
Rachel Humphries, teacher at Westacre Middle School

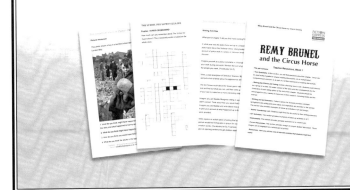

FICTI●N EXPRESS

Rémy Brunel and the Circus Horse
by Sharon Gosling

"Roll up, roll up, and see the greatest show on Earth!" Rémy Brunel loves her life in the circus – riding elephants, practising tightrope tricks and dazzling audiences. But when two new magicians arrive at the circus, everyone is wary of them. What exactly are they up to? What secrets are they trying to hide? Should Rémy and her new friend Matthias trust them?

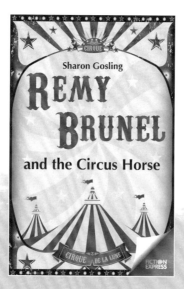

ISBN 978-1-78322-469-2

FICTION EXPRESS

The Time Detectives:
The Mystery of Maddie Musgrove
by Alex Woolf

When Joe Smallwood goes to stay with his Uncle Theo
and cousin Maya life seems dull, until he finds a strange
smartphone nestling beside a gravestone. The phone
enables Joe and Maya to become time-travelling detectives
and takes them on an exciting adventure back to Victorian
times. Can they prove maidservant Maddie Musgrove's
innocence? Can they save her from the gallows?

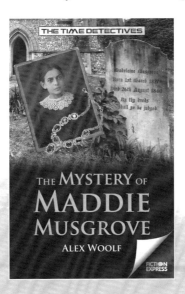

ISBN 978-1-78322-459-3

FICTI●N EXPRESS

The Time Detectives:
The Disappearance of Danny Doyle
by Alex Woolf

When the Time Detectives, Joe and Maya, stumble upon an old house in the middle of a wood, its occupant has a sad tale to tell. Michael was evacuated to Dorset during World War II with his twin brother, Danny. While there, Danny mysteriously disappeared and was never heard from again. Can Joe and Maya succeed where the police failed, journey back to 1941 and trace Michael's missing brother?

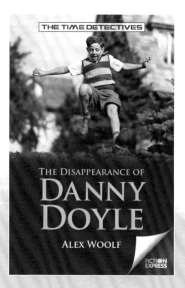

ISBN 978-1-78322-458-6

FICTION EXPRESS

The Sand Witch
by Tommy Donbavand

When twins Chris and Ella are left to look after
their younger brother on a deserted beach, they
expect everything to be normal, boring in fact. But
then something extraordinary happens! Will the
Sand Witch succeed in passing on her sandy curse
in this exciting adventure?

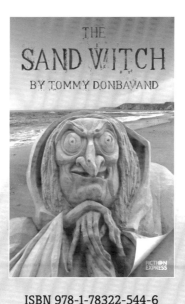

ISBN 978-1-78322-544-6

About the Author

Prizewinning author Stewart Ross taught at all levels in Britain, the USA, the Middle East and Sri Lanka before becoming a full-time writer twenty-six years ago. Some 280 (lost count) of his books have been published, including two novels for adults and 35 works of fiction for children. He has written plays, lyrics and poetry, too. His books have been translated into around 20 languages.

When not writing, Stewart enjoys travel, music, sport, theatre and ambling through the woods near his home. As a change from the large garden hut in which he works, Stewart ventures forth to schools, colleges and universities in Britain, France and elsewhere to talk about writing and pass on his passion for words.